MW01014709

Find the THREE WORDS hidden
in the pictures of this book
and discover the three powers needed
to unlock the magic of the tea.
Enter the words and see the story come to life at:

booksicals.com/magicteahouse/powers

I start every writing session with a cup of tea. It quiets my spirit, and much like it does for Hopper Smith, the boy in the book, tea has a magical way of unlocking my imagination. So sip a cup of tea and join me and Tea Master David De Candia for a magical tea adventure.

- Susan Chodakiewitz

In many ways the characters in this book, Hopper Smith and Master Davey, co-exist in me each and every day. I discovered tea sixteen years ago and, like Hopper, every day since then I looked forward to what magic tea will uncover. Much like Master Davey, I love sharing my passion about tea with others. And to make the reading experience more exciting I've created the Blue Tiger Blend inspired by the book. I hope you will share a cup with your family and experience the magic for yourself.

- David De Candia

To Mel Elias whose support has never wavered.
To my family, wife Irma, Robert, Gloriana and Anissa, who have been my cheerleaders during this wonderful journey of tea.

- D.D.

To PZ Miller best listener and friend.

- S.C.

Master Davey and The Magic Tea House

Legend of the Blue Tiger

by
Susan Chodakiewitz
and
David De Candia

Booksicals
A Booksicals® book
published in partnership with
The Coffee Bean & Tea Leaf®
Los Angeles, California

None of the customers at the Magic Tea House actually believed Master Davey's teas were magical... Except for a boy named Hopper Smith.

Day by day Hopper watched Master Davey prepare his magic blends. Sometimes Master Davey added spices or roots or the peel of fruits. Sometimes he added buds or the petals of flowers.

“Take a whiff of my newest blend, Jasmine Dragon Phoenix Pearl. What do you smell, Hopper? What do you smell?”

“A bouquet of flowers... and a summer breeze," said Hopper.

“Getting better, Hopper! Getting better!" said Master Davey.

One day Master Davey took out a mysterious jade box with only a few leaves of tea in it. He steeped the tea and poured Hopper a cup. "What do you smell, Hopper? What do you smell?"

Hopper closed his eyes and took a long deep breath. "I smell the scent of a tiger!" said Hopper.

"Very good, Hopper! Very good!" said Master Davey. "This is the last of the Blue Tiger Tea, the most rare and precious tea of all. And it is about to be lost to the world forever."

"Is there any way to save it?" asked Hopper.

"The legend of the Blue Tiger Tea tells of a boy who will someday save it. Perhaps you are that boy," said Master Davey.

"How do I know if I am?" asked Hopper.

"Do you have the courage to find out?"

Hopper nodded. Master Davey held out the tea cup. Swirls of steam rose up from it.

"Watch the leaves as they uncurl, Hopper, and let the magic of the tea unfurl..."

When the steam cleared, Hopper found himself in a field of scraggly, withered bushes. Beside him stood a girl.

"Where am I?" asked Hopper. "And who are you?"

"I am Camellia. You are in the Blue Tiger Tea fields of my village in Yunnan, China."

"What happened to your tea fields?" asked Hopper.

"The tea moth has destroyed them."

"Can't they be replanted?" asked Hopper.

"We have no seeds left," said Camellia. "Long ago the ancient emperor Shen Nong found my ancestors worthy to be the keepers of his precious Blue Tiger Tea and entrusted them with twelve seeds. We have been growing this tea ever since... But now our fields are dried up. We have failed to protect the tea."

A tear rolled down Camellia's face.

"There must be someplace we can get more seeds," said Hopper.

"The seeds only grow on the emperor's Blue Tiger Tea tree. And no one knows where it is."

"I'll help you find it," said Hopper.

"There is a legend of a boy who will someday save the Blue Tiger Tea. If you are that boy, then perhaps the tea will lead us," said Camellia.

Camellia brought out a pouch of Blue Tiger Tea and a pot of hot water.

"This is the last of the Blue Tiger Tea," said Camellia. She poured it into the pot. Then she took her ceremonial tea scarf from around her neck and placed it on Hopper.

"Wear this for the journey," said Camellia. "It is the sign of the protector of the tea."

Swirls of steam rose up from the pot. Hopper closed his eyes and took a breath...

"What do you smell, Hopper? What do you smell?" asked Camellia.

"I smell the scent of a forest..."

A strong wind arose and swept them to a dense forest in the Himalayas. From behind a tree a woman appeared.

"I am Mihika, the keeper of the Wild Tea Forest...The winds told me to expect you."

"We are in search of the ancient Blue Tiger Tea tree," said Camellia. "Do you know where to find it?"

"It grows in a secret place known only to the ancient emperor Shen Nong," said Mihika.

Trees swayed and leaves spun as the winds grew fiercer.

"We must find the tree!" said Hopper.

"I wish I could help you," said Mihika, "but a monsoon is approaching. I must pluck and gather the youngest leaves or they will be damaged by the wind. And you should be on your way before the storm hits."

"We will stay and help you!" said Camellia.

"It is dangerous work to climb the trees against the treacherous winds," said Mihika.

"If you show us how, we can do it!" said Hopper.

The wind stung their faces and pulled at their clothes while they climbed the trees and picked the tea leaves. And just as they had plucked the very last leaf, the clouds burst and the rain came pouring down.

Mihika hurried them into a small hut. "Thank you for helping me," said Mihika. "You have shown great kindness and true courage."

While the winds howled and the rain hammered, Mihika steeped some tea.

"There is a legend," said Mihika, "that long ago the emperor Shen Nong rested here. He quenched his thirst with the wild tea from the forest. And in gratitude he whispered to the leaves the secret place of the Blue Tiger tree...Listen to the tea and it will lead you to where you have to go," said Mihika.

Swirls of steam rose up from the cups. Hopper closed his eyes and concentrated...

"What do you hear, Hopper? What do you hear?" asked Camellia.

"I hear the chirping of birds and the buzzing of bees..."

The steam wrapped and whirled around them and when it cleared, Hopper and Camellia stood at a golden gate guarded by a big round man with a sword.

"This is the Magic Tea Garden of the ancient emperor Shen Nong! I am Wali, its protector. And YOU are trespassing!"

Camellia bowed. "We mean no disrespect. But we must find the Blue Tiger Tea tree," she said.

"NO ONE is permitted near the Blue Tiger tree. It is guarded by the fierce Blue Tiger!"

"But we must get the seeds to save Camellia's village!" said Hopper.

Wali looked closely at Hopper...

"A legend tells of a boy with the courage to face the Blue Tiger. If you are that boy, then you will know the answer to this question..."

"Beyond this gate are three mountains," said Wali. "One of them conceals the ancient tea tree and the Blue Tiger that guards it. WHICH MOUNTAIN IS IT? If you answer correctly, you wil be granted entrance. But if you err... beware... the garden will spit you out forever."

One mountain was made of gold. The other made of silver. And one was plain and brown. Hopper thought and thought...Then he remembered Master Davey's words...

"Tea leaves appear humble. But their magic lies in their essence..."

"The plain mountain!" said Hopper. "That's the one we choose!"

"Are you sure?" asked Wali.

"Yes," said Hopper. "I am sure."

The gates of the garden swung open.

"You have answered correctly," said Wali. "Now you must face the Blue Tiger!"

A blue mist hovered over the mountain. At the top lurked the Blue Tiger, bigger and fiercer than Hopper and Camellia had imagined. And when the tiger caught sight of them, he let out a terrifying growl.

"He is going to attack us!" said Camellia.

"We must be brave!" said Hopper.

Hopper removed the ceremonial tea scarf that Camellia had given him and slowly approached the tiger... "Great Blue Tiger, Protector of the Tea," said Hopper. "We need your help. Please grant us permission to gather seeds from the tree so that we can save Camellia's village."

Hopper bowed to the tiger, and offered him the scarf.

The Blue Tiger shook and shuffled and ruffled his fur... And before their eyes the great blue beast transformed into the ancient emperor Shen Nong!

"Your Majesty!" said Camellia. She bowed to the emperor and yanked Hopper down beside her.

"You showed kindness by helping Mihika and wisdom by correctly answering Wali's question," said the emperor. "And now you have faced the tiger with great courage. You have proven that you are truly worthy to be a protector of the tea."

"Now, Camellia, take this pouch with twelve new seeds and bring them back to your village. When the first growth is ready for harvesting, give Hopper a seedling with two leaves and a bud. He has earned the privilege to be a keeper of the Blue Tiger Tea."

The emperor turned and walked away. Then he faded into a blue mist.

When the mist cleared, they were standing in Camellia's village.

"Father! We have brought you seeds from the ancient Blue Tiger Tea tree!"

"We must plant them at once!" said Camellia's father.

Together they dug twelve holes. Hopper and Camellia placed one seed in each hole and covered the seeds with earth.

"We must be patient," said Camellia's father. "It will take seven years before the tea can be harvested."

But as they watered the seeds, new tea bushes started to grow. In minutes, the fields were lush and green again.

"You have saved our village!" said Camellia's father.

Together they gathered the first leaves from the newly sprouted fields. Then they soaked the leaves and dried them and prepared them for steeping.

And when the leaves were ready, Camellia handed Hopper the seedling with two leaves and a bud as the emperor had commanded. She smiled. "You really are the boy from the legend," she said.

Camellia poured Hopper a cup of tea. The steam from the cup whirled around him.

"Taste the tea, Hopper," said Camellia.

And the instant the tea touched Hopper's lips he heard a familiar voice...

"Welcome back, Hopper!" said Master Davey. Hopper looked around and realized he was back at the Magic Tea House.

"I did it, Master Davey! I did it! I saved the Blue Tiger Tea!" Hopper handed Master Davey the seedling with two leaves and a bud.

"I see the emperor has found you worthy to be a keeper of the Blue Tiger Tea!"

Master Davey smiled. "Now tell me, Hopper, how was your journey?"

"Magical, Master Davey. Absolutely magical!"

Believe

I have the privilege of working alongside many wonderful and caring team members at The Coffee Bean & Tea Leaf®, but none more than David De Candia (or Master Davey). David is the most passionate and knowledgeable person about tea I have ever known.

David could write any book about tea, but he specifically wanted to write a children's book so he could truly capture the magical journey that each tea origin evokes -- the very same journey he experiences each time he tastes a new blend or variety.

I hope this book, inspired by David's personal experiences, awakens the passion for tea in you. May your tea adventures begin!

Mel Elias, CEO
The Coffee Bean & Tea Leaf®

Published by Booksicals® in partnership
with *The Coffee Bean & Tea Leaf®* in Los Angeles, California

Copyright © 2013
by Susan Chodakiewitz and *The Coffee Bean & Tea Leaf®*
All rights reserved.

Library of Congress Control Number 2012923729
ISBN 13: 978-0-9886970-0-3

1. Tea - Juvenile 2. Tiger-Legend 3. Magic Journey 4. Emperor Shen Nong
5. Courage

Summary: Hopper Smith, a boy with the power to unlock the hidden stories inside every cup of tea, must save the precious Blue Tiger Tea from disappearing from the world forever.

The text of this book is set in Archer and Channel Left Slanted

CPSIA Compliance Information: Batch # 0213.
For further information contact:
RJ Communications, NY, NY, 1-800-621-2556.
Printed in USA

The illustrations are hand-drawn with digital color.

The Coffee Bean & Tea Leaf® name and logo are registered trademarks of
International Coffee & Tea, LLC.

DESIGN: by Kent Yoshimura, Los Angeles, California

For more books by Booksicals® visit:
booksicals.com

For more information about *The Coffee Bean & Tea Leaf®* visit:
coffeebean.com

Every tea has a story...